THE GLASS BOY

BY MELAINA FARANDA
ILLUSTRATED BY STEFAN MESSAM

heBET

"Sewer Rat, you little bonehead, do you want my arms to burn off? Bring me the cutters!"

Throwing down the iron poker, Pietro left off stoking the furnace to hasten to his master with the glass cutters. He put a grimy hand over his mouth to hide a yawn. They had been working all night. Already a pale beam of light was creeping through the stone slits near the foundry roof. Soon the bells would peal for the people of Venice to rise and hurry to work.

But still Maestro Battono refused to sleep. Pietro knew why. In less than a week, their fate would be decided.

PREDICT

What time period do you think this story is set in? What helped you form your opinion?

PIETRO SHUDDERED AT THE THOUGHT of what had happened at the meeting of the Glass Masters only the day before. The meeting had been long and boring and his master had become drunk. Maestro Battono had insulted Maestro Mancini, who had in turn challenged him to a bet.

…ho made the most exquisite piece for the Doge to carry in the procession on Murano … would win the other's foundry. The loser would surrender the right to work as …aster ever again.

Pietro had begged his master to think of Isabella, but Maestro Battono had flicked him off like a flea from a dog. He had sworn an oath on his foundry, the Golden Book and Saint Anthony. The Golden Book was the book in which the noble families of Venice were recorded. It was the same book that appeared in the paws of the winged lion that decorated all of Venice. Saint Anthony was the patron saint of glass-blowers.

…e Doge were prepared to overlook a blasphemy on the Golden Book, the glass-blowers …er let an oath sworn on Saint Anthony be broken.

MAESTRO BATTONO HAD SEALED THEIR FATE

BEYOND THE TEXT

Research:
The Golden Book of Venice
– real or imaginary?

VISUAL FEATURES

What effects do the visual images and design have on you? How do these features influence your first impressions of Pietro's life in the glass foundry?

THE APPRENTICE

Maestro Battono could not hold his wine. Pietro knew he should be thankful for that. His own fortunes had relied upon the master being drunk.

It had only been with glazed eyes and a slur in his voice that the maestro had allowed a sickly woman in rags to address him – a great master of glass! With her brood of wailing children clustered about her, the woman had pressed her half-starved boy upon him. Back then, Pietro's work had been to dive into the canal and find dropped items to sell.

HE STANK OF SEWAGE.

Maestro Battono had wrinkled his nose.

"PLEASE, GREAT MAESTRO, TAKE HIM,"

Pietro's mother had begged.

"He is a good boy, but there is no food. He will work hard for you. Please, I beg you."

VISUAL FEATURES

What hidden messages are conveyed in the images? Why do you think the illustrator has shown the contrasts in lighting?

CLARIFY

brood

woman in rags

READING BETWEEN THE LINES

Why do you think the author included details of Pietro's impoverished family? Is there an underlying reason here? Why do you think this?

LANGUAGE FEATURES

Simile/Metaphor/Personification/Alliteration

What literary devices has the author used here?
Why do you think she has used them?
How did it help you create a mental image?

FOR SIX YEARS NOW, PIETRO HAD SLAVED for Maestro Battono. He had fetched alder wood. He had carted limestone, arsenic, plantash and silica. He had learned that the best silica stones were from Istria and the next best were those from Ticino River.

He had been taught not to be tricked by stones from Verona that would make the glass yellow. Even the master's jealously guarded formulas for producing different glass – crystalline, enamel, multi-coloured, milk-glass, glass with threads of gold – had been revealed to him. Now, if the master didn't make the most wonderful glass object, IT WOULD ALL HAVE BEEN FOR NOTHING.

SETTING

How effectively has the author described the glasswork foundry and the glassmaking process of the time? Is the historical context credible? Why/why not?

"Bah!" Maestro Battono spat, jolting Pietro from his gloomy thoughts. "It's no good. See how the glass cools too quickly!" He thrust it back into the blazing hole and then pulled it out again.

With one hand, Maestro Battono kept hold of the pole capped with a fiery molten blob. With the other, he deftly tweaked the glowing ball with the tweezer-like cutters.

Pietro knew he should continue to stack alder wood. Instead, he moved silently into the red-lit shadows of the foundry. He was unable to take his eyes off the magic taking place in front of him.

BEYOND THE TEXT

Can you relate to Pietro's fascination with the art of glassmaking? What connections can you make?

Ever since he had arrived here as a frightened child, without his family, only a rough sacking pallet in the foundry for his bed, and a gruff master who barked orders and called him Sewer Rat, PIETRO HAD BEEN ENCHANTED BY GLASS.

His world inside the foundry was grimy, dark and hot. That a gritty mix of sand, lime and soda could become silky glass in such a setting seemed a miracle.

The Glass Master grimly pulled the glass into shape, flipping toffee-like tentacles of aventurine glass over and over. When the piece grew too hard, he plunged it back into the blazing heat to soften it. It began to resemble a confectionery crown.

"Look, Sewer Rat," Maestro Battono grunted, sensing Pietro watching from the shadows. "This crown is to represent the power of La Serenissima, our most Serene Republic of Venice, for the Doge to carry in the procession."

Pietro gazed at the crown. It was very beautiful. But how could they know if it was the best?

CLARIFY

limestone
arsenic
plantash
silica
aventurine glass

THE GOLDEN BOOK

"You know that, if I were to lose, I could never leave Venice," Maestro Battono said.

Pietro nodded. After six long years, he knew his master well. Maestro Battono was not asking a question. He was thinking aloud.

"They would cut off my hands or have me killed. It is the law. No glassmaker may leave Venice, in case we share our secrets with other nations."

This was indeed very harsh, but who, Pietro secretly thought, would ever wish to leave Venice?

"And my daughter would not be able to marry into the nobility," the maestro continued.

At this mention of Isabella, Pietro's heart leapt against his ribs. Isabella was the only one who had ever shown kindness to him. When her father was out on business, Isabella sometimes crept into the foundry. Encouraged by her laughter, Pietro told her stories. Tales about living in stacked wooden slums on stinking canals that were only a short gondola ride away, but which she would never see.

"IT IS A PRIVILEGE OF GLASSMAKERS ALONE," Maestro Battono continued. "Because we are so important to the Republic. It will be a proud day when I see Isabella living with her noble in a palazzo on the Grand Canal. My grandchildren's names will be written into the Golden Book."

Pietro looked intently into the furnace. Of course, he knew that this was what would happen. He was only a lowly servant. He should never have even dreamed...

Maestro Battono gazed at the cooled piece. He turned it over and shook his head. "It is not good enough."

HE HURLED IT AGAINST THE WALL.

ISSUES

Pietro thinks of himself as only a lowly servant. What is your view on the issue of social prejudice? How can people avoid social prejudice today?

They would cut off my hands or have me killed. It is the law.

CLARIFY

nobility
gondola
palazzo

INFERENCE

Pietro wonders, "Who would ever wish to leave Venice?" What inferences can you make from this?

BROKEN DREAMS

The broken crown lay shattered on the stone floor.

Pietro stared miserably as Maestro Battono tore off his apron and stalked from the foundry. He knew his master had gone to the tavern. The scullery maid had whispered that the master had started to drink too much the year before Pietro had arrived, after his beloved wife and Isabella's mother had died of the plague.

There was something sad about the glittering shards, as if they were the fragments of a broken dream. Unable to bear the waste, Pietro swept the broken glass into a wooden pail. He tipped it into a crucible and slid it into the furnace.

When the glass was liquid again, Pietro pulled it out of the furnace. He stuck in a pole to draw out, like magic, a red-hot, glowing lump.

Idly tweaking the glass with the cutters, Pietro allowed whatever came into his imagination to take shape.

HE HAD LEARNED, LONG AGO, THAT THE GLASS MUST TELL HIM WHAT IT WISHED TO BE.

Four legs were conjured, a snaking tail and a heart-shaped head with slanting eyes and triangle ears. Pietro laid the piece carefully upon the slab of cooling granite and stood it upright: a small glass cat. It was not just one of the thousands of cats that lazed on balconies or prowled the fish market. This was Isabella's cat: Leone, the little lion, right down to the haughty twitch of its tail.

CLARIFY

- scullery maid
- shards
- crucible
- granite
- haughty

CHARACTER ANALYSIS

Summarise what you know about Pietro and Maestro Battono.

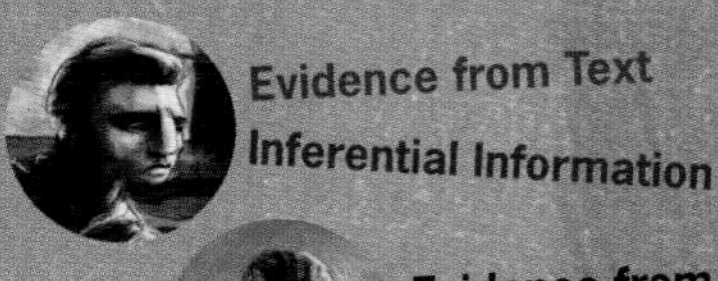

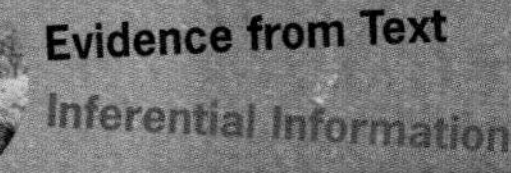

Plot

Is the plot convincing in your opinion? Why/why not? What do you think will happen in the story now?

Pietro longed to see the tiny dimple that would form in Isabella's left cheek as she smiled at the miniature glass Leone. He had given her such gifts before, but always with the unspoken understanding that she must not mention them to her father. Pietro was sometimes permitted to do lesser work when his master was too busy. He would make up an order for lantern glass or cheap beads for the bead stringers.

Maestro Battono did not know that his Sewer Rat practised glass-blowing in secret.

Pietro gazed at the haughty little cat. He wrapped it tenderly in a square of cloth. Isabella would never receive this gift of love.

Now Pietro thought about his mother and brothers and sisters. They lived in one cramped room, infested with cockroaches and rats, surviving solely on his tiny wage.

If Maestro Battono lost the bet,

What would happen to them all?

Symbolism

What symbolic reference can you find in this text? What connections can you make to the underlying meaning?

BURNS MARK THE TRADE

"Pietro! What are you doing here?" A range of expressions darted across his mother's lined face. Shock. Pleasure. Shame. "It is not Sunday."

It was true. Pietro was kept busy by Maestro Battono. He only ever visited on a Sunday, when he was given the morning off to attend church. His mother was always waiting. There would be a stew of SLIMY FISH HEADS that made him gag.

CLARIFY

gag
bellissimo

Still, he bravely spooned it down so that, like every Venetian mamma, she could beam with pleasure at feeding him.

Today, his mother had been caught unprepared. Beyond the narrow door, a suffocating smell wafted up. The baby lay in its own filth, screaming.

A shadowy rat scrambled up a mildewed wall and out through the single tiny window. Pietro hugged his mother and felt the sharpness of her bones beneath her ragged dress. She drew away and caught his hands to examine them. "So many new burns!"

Pietro shrugged. "BURNS MARK THE TRADE," he said proudly. It was something that glass-blowers showed off about.

"Pietro! Pietro!" The children came running from further up the narrow alley and threw themselves upon him. He felt their sharp little limbs twist around him. His heart ached that they should be so thin. "What have you brought us?" cheeky Celestina demanded.

VISUAL FEATURES

Why do you think the illustrator used "cold" colours? How does this influence your response to the story? Why do you think the illustrator has highlighted Pietro's family using a different lighting effect?

Pietro grinned. Sometimes he brought them glass beads that his master had rejected. Beads that were misshapen or had blotchy patterns. He drew out the square of cloth and opened it to reveal the glass cat.

"Oh, Pietro, it is bellissimo!" Celestina cried. She reached out her grubby fingers to touch it.

Pietro swooped it out of reach. "No. This must be sold. Mamma, you can get some money for this. You will need it. I might not be working for Maestro Battono much longer."

PERSONAL RESPONSE

What feelings are evoked by the author's description of Pietro's family and the adversities they face?

THE DISASTER

Pietro wandered slowly back along the watery green streets. Washing flapped from balconies. Hawkers shouted out above the clink of boats to buy their fish, freshly caught from the blue sea beyond the Lido. Pietro breathed in the pungent odours of brine, sewage, rotting wood, fish and frying doughnuts. THE SMELL OF VENICE. THE SMELL OF HOME.

CLARIFY
hawkers
pungent
brine
masterpiece
coax

He felt heavy with the memory of his mother's tears. He should not have told her about the bet. The truth was, Maestro Battono was a master with glass. Pietro had absorbed every one of his many secrets and techniques. There was no reason why Maestro Battono should not create a masterpiece worthy of the Doge.

Except that he drank too much.

SETTING
How credible is the author's description of Venice. What helped her form the historical perspective? What information do you need to assess the authenticity of the setting?

With sudden determination, Pietro knew that he must find his master and coax him from the tavern. He would work beside him, day and night, fetching and carrying and lifting and clearing, without complaint. He would help Maestro Battono create the finest glass object in all of Venice!

He raced to the tavern.

There ahead of him, almost stumbling into the canal, was his master.

"Pietro..." Maestro Battono looked up groggily then bent double. He groaned in agony.

Something was terribly wrong. Pietro hurried forward. He should never have gone to see his family. He should have raced after his master the moment he stalked from the foundry.

"The wine..." Maestro Battono choked out. "Tasted strange... Mancini's men were there. I think I have been pois..."

HE COLLAPSED.

CHARACTER ANALYSIS
"He felt heavy with the memory of his mother's tears."
How do you think Pietro could be feeling? Why do you think this?

LANGUAGE FEATURES

Why has the author introduced Italian terms such as "Doge" in the text? What is the purpose of this?

the finest glass object in all of Venice

LANGUAGE AND VISUAL FEATURES

What effect does the choice of language, design and visual images have on you? How do these features enhance your interpretation of the story?

A SICK MAN

CLARIFY
ducat
footman
gondolier
apothecary

Pietro hammered the lion knocker on the great wooden door of the villa. On the promise of a ducat, another man had helped him to carry Maestro Battono home.

The door flew open and Isabella appeared behind the maid. When she saw her father, Isabella's face turned whiter than milk-glass. "Pietro. What is wrong? What has happened?"

"He was outside the tavern."

A knowing look was exchanged between them.

"But it is not what you think," Pietro added. "HE SAID SOMETHING ABOUT POISON."

Isabella turned back into the house and screamed, "Franco! Giovanni!"

There was a clatter of footsteps as Maestro Battono's footman and gondolier rushed out and seized their master. "Take him to his bed chamber!" Isabella commanded. "Pietro, will you fetch the apothecary?"

He nodded and dashed off.

By the time Pietro returned with the apothecary, Maestro Battono was laid out between fine Damascus sheets. His face was grey.

"Will he live?" Isabella whispered. Tears streaked her cheeks.

Pietro's heart twisted.

The apothecary looked grim. "He is a very sick man. I cannot say."

Pietro stared at his master, horrified. Isabella had not been told about the bet. If she lost her father, she would lose the foundry and, with it, all her chances for a good marriage. He could not bear to think of her living in a hovel like his mother, sad and thin.

OPINION
Do you think Isabella should have been told about the bet? Why/why not?

CLARIFY

luminous
serpentine
masonry

Luminous shadows

Luminous Shadows

Back in the foundry, Pietro sat amid the vats of potash and silica, despairing. His thoughts turned, as always, to glass.

The most wonderful glass object...

Pietro thought about Venice and all the things he loved. The play of light on the water. Its shifting greens and luminous shadows. The serpentine swirl of water beneath the gondolier's silent oars. The rings of light dancing out when he tossed a stone into the canal.

Then there were the winged lions of San Marco. They had been worked into the masonry above every grand building and in every public square. The big brass lion's head knockers upon the carved wooden doors. Isabella and her Leone, her little lion...

Messages

What messages do you think the author is trying to convey about the relationship between Pietro and Isabella?

The play of light on the water

Reading between the lines

What inferences can you make about Pietro's thoughts and the direction the plot is taking?

THE MASTER

Feverishly, Pietro mixed the correct amounts of soda, zinc, calcium carbonate, lime and silica, measuring each with exactness.

He knew how to make ruby, purple, aqua, topaz, cobalt, emerald, teal, yellow and a hundred shades in between.

CLARIFY
calcium carbonate
topaz
cobalt
teal

The lowest furnace blazed with the alder wood he had stacked only the day before. He put in the crucible.

When the glass was liquid, Pietro pulled it out on the pole and began to work it with the cutters and other tools. As he worked, he thought about Isabella and his mother, THE WINGED GLORY OF VENICE AND ITS JEWEL-COLOURED CANALS.

Holding his breath, Pietro teased out strips, layer by layer. Fusing the colours was a challenge, as some set hard earlier than others.

At last, Pietro laid his creation upon the granite to cool. He watched it harden in the orange firelight.

It was finished. Pietro picked it up and anxiously checked for any hidden flaws.

BEYOND THE TEXT
What connections can you make to Pietro's desire to create a perfect work of art?

Were there any dull spots where ash had stuck to it while it was cooling? Or bubbles that had expanded from the colourant? There could be no paper burns or chill marks, no cracks, holes, nicks or scratches.

He placed it back on the granite and stared in wonder.

It was perfect.

QUESTION

What do you think is meant by **"the** winged glory of Venice"?

JUDGEMENT DAY

The Glass Masters' meeting was more crowded than Pietro had ever seen it before.

Maestro Battono was still in bed, unable to rise. He was certain he had lost the bet and refused to speak of it. It was as if he thought he could simply close his eyes and make it all go away.

Carefully, Pietro picked his way through the crowd.

CLARIFY

casket
gravest duty
galleon
signori

Maestro Mancini already sat at the head table with his own casket placed in front of him. He looked surprised. "Where is Maestro Battono?" He pronounced Battono as if he had bitten a raw onion.

"My master is unwell this morning," Pietro declared. "He sent me in his place to bring the Doge's glass."

Maestro Mancini scowled.

The head of the Glass Masters' meeting gestured everyone to silence. "Signori, today we must do the gravest duty. One man stands to lose his foundry and profession. We must uphold the standards of the Glass Masters of the Serene Republic of Venice. There can be no decision made from friendship or rivalry. It will be your duty to select the finest piece to be presented for the Doge's procession in Murano. Maestro Mancini, will you please present your piece?"

It was more than the heat of an overcrowded room that made Pietro sweat as the maestro drew out his piece very slowly, for greater effect.

SIGHS OF ADMIRATION GREETED IT.

It was a miniature galleon, complete with sails and rigging and oars, spun from crystalline glass.

Maestro Mancini looked smug. He turned the galleon to show off its workmanship. "This is to represent the mighty wealth of Venice as a trading republic."

The head Glass Master looked sympathetically at Pietro, as if the winner had already been clearly decided. "Let us now see Maestro Battono's work."

Pietro carefully unwrapped the cloth and then pulled away another finer layer – a silk handkerchief that Isabella had given him.

This time the room was so silent, Pietro could hear Maestro Mancini's intake of breath.

The Glass Master's face turned purple with mottled fury, then white with fear.

INFERENCE

"This time the room was so silent…"

What inferences can you make from this?

READING BETWEEN THE LINES

What would the consequences be for Pietro and Maestro Battono if the Glass Masters discovered that Pietro made the glasswork for the competition?

SYMBOLISM

How appropriate are the symbolic references to Venice in Pietro's glasswork? Are the references specific enough? Why/why not?

THE WINGED LION

Pietro gazed at his creation.

The winged lion shimmered in the lamplight. Individual threads of gold swirled through its mane in perfect harmony. Every contour of its muscular body was embraced by light.

THE LION GAZED DOWN SERENELY, AS IF GUARDING A SACRED POSSESSION.

Nestled between its upturned paws was a bowl. It contained twisting strands of colour: the white-green of morning light upon the canals, the blue-green depths of midday, the gold-green of afternoon and the silvery purple-blue of a moonlit night.

"This is San Marco's winged lion," Pietro cried, "forever protecting the Republic of Venice!"

CLARIFY

harmony
contour
serenely

AUTHOR PURPOSE

How has the author shown a change in Pietro's character from earlier descriptions of him? Why do you think the author has done this?

The winged
shimmered
in the lampli

When Maestro Battono was well enough to sit up, Isabella told him what had happened. He demanded to see the winged lion and was told he must wait until he could visit the Doge's palace.

A month later, he visited. And afterwards he sought Pietro out in the foundry.

Pietro looked up, half afraid, from where he was patiently stacking more firewood.

HIS MASTER WOULD NOW KNOW THAT HE HAD BEEN PRACTISING IN SECRET.

I have seen it. I should be angry, but how can I
e maestro leaned heavily upon his stick. "I have
inking about this foundry of Mancini's. Seems a
not to use it, and I have no sons…"

aestro!" In a flash, Pietro saw how it could be. He could create whatever he chose
d build a fortune. He would train his brothers and there would be money for his
ther and sisters to eat good food and wear fine dresses. Perhaps one day he
ght even be worthy of Isabella…

"You're a good boy," said the maestro. Then he added gruffly, "FOR A SEWER RAT."

QUESTION GENERATE

What questions can you ask?

READING BETWEEN THE LINES

How has the relationship between the maestro and Pietro changed? Will social prejudice still influence the way Pietro sees himself? Why/why not?

PERSONAL RESPONSE

What helped you relate to the events in this story?

He could create whatever he chose and build a fortune.

SETTING

Analyse the elements that help you form an impression of the canal slums where Pietro's family live.

Description of Place in Text

Illustrative Description

Impact on Characters

Mood/Atmosphere

THINK ABOUT THE TEXT

MAKING CONNECTIONS

What connections can you make to the characters, plot, setting and themes of *The Glass Boy*?

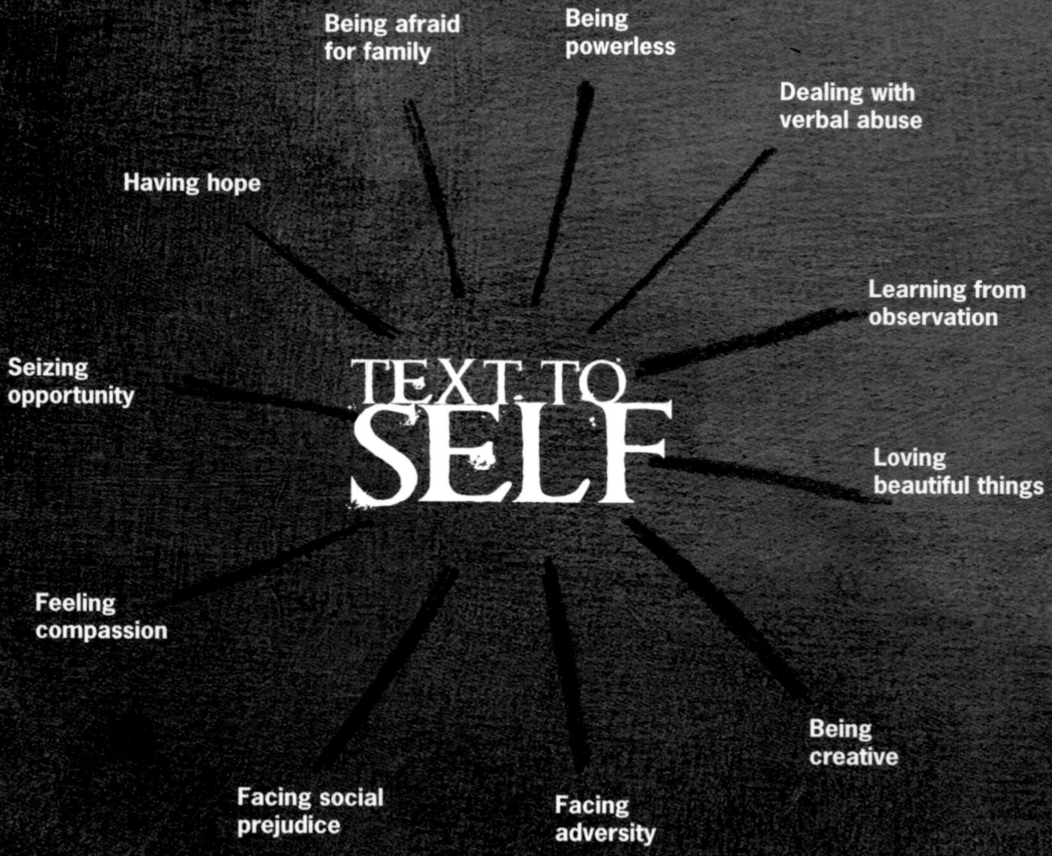

TEXT TO SELF

- Being afraid for family
- Being powerless
- Dealing with verbal abuse
- Learning from observation
- Loving beautiful things
- Being creative
- Facing adversity
- Facing social prejudice
- Feeling compassion
- Seizing opportunity
- Having hope

TEXT TO TEXT/ MEDIA

Talk about texts/media you have read, listened to or seen that have similar themes and compare the treatment of theme and the differing author styles.

TEXT TO WORLD

Talk about situations in the world that might connect to elements in the story.

PLANNING AN HISTORICAL FICTION

THINK ABOUT WHAT DEFINES HISTORICAL FICTION

Historical fiction connects the reader with the situations and events of history. It incorporates an historical period and historical events as a background for the thoughts and actions of characters – fictitious or real.

THINK ABOUT THE PLOT

Decide on a plot that has an introduction, problems and a solution, and write them in the order of sequence.

Build your story to a turning point. This is the most exciting/suspenseful part of the story.

Decide on an event to draw the reader into your story. What will the main conflict/problem be?

Climax

Conflict

Falling Action

Decide on a final event that will resolve the conflict/problem and bring your story to a close.

Set the scene: who is the story about? When and where is it set?

Introduction

Resolution

Think about the sequence of events and how to present them using researched knowledge of the historical time frame.

THINK ABOUT THE CHARACTERS

Explore:

- how characters from the chosen historical time frame think, feel and act

- what motivates their behaviour
- the social structures that affect their status and behaviour.

DECIDE ON THE SETTING

Atmosphere/mood → location → time

Think about the setting and how to present it using researched knowledge of the historical time frame.

Note: Historical fiction is usually set in one period of time or explores one aspect of history.

WRITING AN HISTORICAL FICTION

HAVE YOU...

- Made links to the society and events of your period?
- Maintained historical accuracy about actual events or settings?
- Been true to the context of your time frame?
- Provided a window on the past?
- Explored the values and beliefs of the time?
- Developed characters that will stand up to in-depth analysis?

...DON T FORGET TO REVISIT YOUR WRITING. DO YOU NEED TO CHANGE, ADD OR DELETE ANYTHING TO IMPROVE YOUR STORY?